CHILD OF
DESTINY

*Child of Destiny*
Copyright © 2008 by Funnypages Productions, LLC

*Requests for information should be addressed to:*
Zondervan, Grand Rapids, Michigan 49530

**Library of Congress Cataloging-in-Publication Data**
Krueger, Jim.
Child of destiny / written by Jim Krueger ; illustrated by Ariel Padilla ; created by Tom Bancroft and Rob Corley.
        p. cm. -- (Tomo book ; v. 3)
    ISBN-13: 978-0-310-71302-9 (softcover)
    ISBN-10: 0-310-71302-1 (softcover)
    1. Graphic novels. I. Padilla, Ariel, 1968- II. Title.
    PN6727.K74C45 2008
    741.5'973--dc22
                                                                    2007031183

This book published in conjunction with Funnypages Productions, LLC, 106 Mission Court, Suite 704, Franklin, TN 37067

Series Editor: Bud Rogers
Managing Editor: Bruce Nuffer
Managing Art Director: Merit Alderink

Printed in United States
08 09 10 11 • 5 4 3 2 1

# CHILD OF DESTINY

SERIES EDITOR
BUD ROGERS

STORY BY
JIM KRUEGER

ART BY
ARIEL PADILLA

funnypages
PRODUCTIONS

ZONDERVAN®

ZONDERVAN.com/
AUTHORTRACKER
follow your favorite authors

# EXAM

NAME: HANA AKISAME
MR. GOLDBERG'S CLASS

1. Mary wants to find the average width of a fourth grader's hand. Which is the best measurement for her to use?
   a. grams
   b. centimeters
   c. meters
   d. kilometers

2. What unit of measure should be used to measure a pencil?
   a. centimeter
   b. kilometer
   c. meter
   d. foot

3. Sharon is measuring how much matter is in her box of animal crackers. What measurement is she making?
   a. volume
   b. height
   c. mass
   d. temperature

4. Fred is 5 feet 7 inches tall. What is Fred's height in inches?
   a. 67 inches
   b. 65 inches
   c. 61 inches

5. The thermometer shows tha
   would the temperature if it w
   a. -10 C
   b. -3 C

I DON'T KNOW WHAT TO SAY...

YOU CAN TALK?

WE ARE COMMANDED TO REST...

...IF ONLY TO MAKE CERTAIN WE ARE NOT CONSUMED BY THE MATTERS OF THE DAY.

CONSUMED LIKE ARDATH.

ARDATH...

ARDATH, AGAIN?

YES.

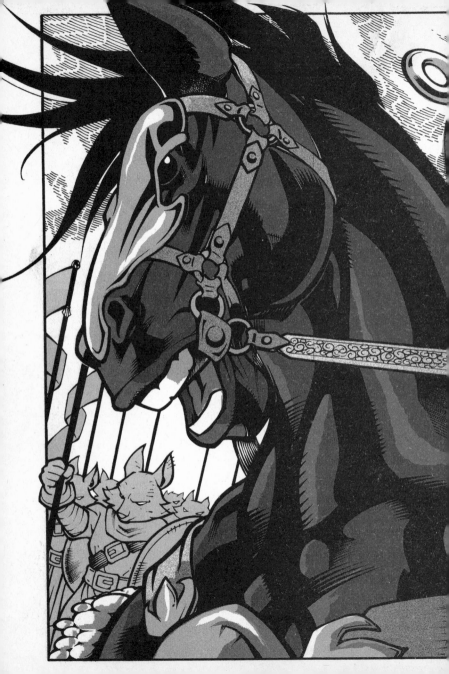

YOU'RE CRYING, TOMO.

AAAK

...NOW ...I CAN'T... BREATHE...

SORRY. I THOUGHT YOU WERE HURTING.

I AM HURTING.

JUST AS TRUTH MUST BE TIMED, HANA, SO TOO MUST COMPASSION BE GIVEN IN THE PROPER WAY.

I WAS JUST TRYING TO HELP.

TOMO LOOKED SAD.

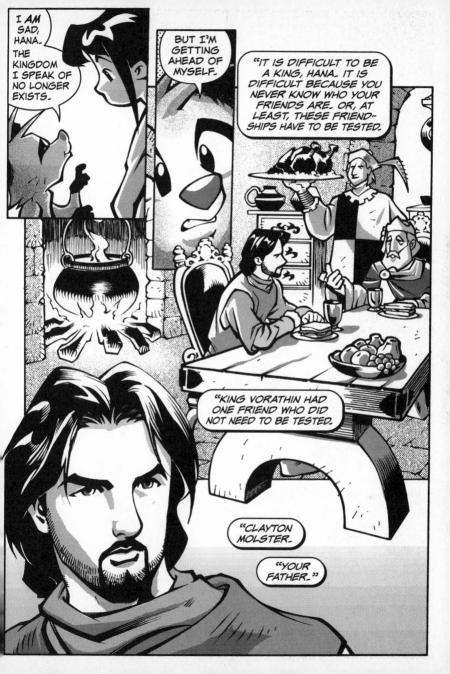

YOU'RE POOR, WHEN YOU COULD BE RICH.

YOU'RE WEAK, WHEN YOU COULD BE STRONG.

YOU'RE SIMPLE, WHEN YOU COULD BE KNOWLEDGE-ABLE.

WHAT IS IT, BROTHER?

I DON'T KNOW, PALON. A WISE MAN, I THINK.

LET'S LISTEN.

A TERRIBLE DAY IS COMING, MY FRIENDS. A DAY OF GREAT DARKNESS WILL SOON COME UPON ARGON FALLS.

QUIET, PALON. IF YOU AND I ARE TO BE KING, WE'RE GOING TO NEED SUCH WISDOM.

FATHER'S ADVISOR CLAYTON IS WISE.

AND CLAYTON DOESN'T TELL FATHER TO MISTRUST THOSE WHO LOVE HIM. HE DOESN'T TURN FATHER AGAINST YOU AND ME.

THAT'S NOT WHAT'S HAPPENING, PALON.

SOMETHING IS NOT RIGHT HERE, ARDATH. YOU MUST LISTEN TO ME.

I DON'T UNDERSTAND. WHO IS THIS URN'ADO?

HANA... NO ONE IS SURE WHERE URN'ADO CAME FROM. SOME SAY FROM THE EAST, BUT THERE ARE OTHERS WHO SAY HE CAME FROM THE SKY. THE ONLY THING THAT THEY KNEW FOR SURE WAS THAT HE CAME WITH WORDS AND IDEAS THAT CAPTIVATED THE PEOPLE OF ARGON FALLS.

HE SPOKE IN A WAY THAT TOUCHED EACH PERSON'S DARKEST NATURE.

HE DECEIVED THE PEOPLE OF ARGON FALLS.

BUT THEY WERE HAPPY. YOU SAID SO.

YES, BUT THE PEOPLE SOON FORGOT WHAT THEY HAD.

PANT... PANT... PANT

HE DIDN'T DECEIVE ALL THE PEOPLE.

YOU MAY BE MY FATHER'S ADVISOR, BUT YOU ARE NOT MINE.

I HATE ARDATH!

HOW COULD HE SAY THAT TO MY FATHER?

HOW!?!

HANA...

...PERHAPS WE WERE WRONG TO THINK YOU WERE READY FOR THIS STORY.

I'M SORRY. PLEASE. TELL THE REST OF THE STORY, TOMO.

"LET US BEGIN TO TALK ABOUT HOW YOUR MOTHER FOUND HERSELF IN ARGON FALLS."

"WHEN SHE WAS YOUNG, HANA, YOUR MOTHER WAS VERY BEAUTIFUL. SHE LIVED NEAR THE MOUNTAINS IN JAPAN. SHE LIVED IN THE TOWN OF OSAKA.

"HER FATHER, YOUR GRANDFATHER JOU, IN THOSE DAYS WAS KNOWN AS A HUNTER, A TRACKER OF LOST MEN. HE WORKED FOR THE POLICE.

"LIKE HER FATHER, YOUR MOTHER WAS TRACKING SOMETHING THAT DAY.

"A PUPPY.

WHIMPERRR

...THROUGH
HERE...
...OH!

THRUD

SMASH

I'LL DROP YOU OFF IN THE VILLAGE.

HERE YOU ARE.

BUT I DON'T LIVE HERE.

THEN, MY DEAR, WHERE DO YOU LIVE?

I'M NOT EVEN SURE HOW I GOT HERE. I WAS CHASING A PUPPY I THOUGHT WAS LOST IN THE WOODS.

I PASSED SOME ARCHES CARVED IN STONE, AND EVERYTHING WENT WHITE.

BEFORE I KNEW IT, I WAS SURROUNDED BY THOSE STONE CREATURES.

ARCHES? A SECRET ENTRANCE?

HER HOME IS NOT IN ARGON FALLS, BUT SOME PLACE CALLED...

...JAPAN?

I'VE NEVER HEARD OF THIS OTHER LAND BEFORE. IS IT BEYOND OUR BORDERS?

CAN YOU HELP HER?

AS YOU KNOW, CLAYTON, THERE IS A SECRET ENTRANCE TO THIS REALM.

BUT NO ONE HAS EVER PASSED THROUGH FROM THE "OTHER WORLD" BEFORE.

SO HOW COULD SHE HAVE COME THROUGH?

UNLESS THE ENTRANCE HAD ALREADY BEEN OPENED...

SIRE? HOW DO WE GET THIS GIRL BACK TO HER HOME AND FAMILY?

A GOOD KING MUST BE MERCIFUL AT TIMES, OR HE WILL BE CONSIDERED A TYRANT.

AND I AM A GOOD KING.

I MUST BE CAUTIOUS. MY PEOPLE, EVEN THOSE CLOSEST TO ME, ARE WEAK AND CAN BE MISTAKEN AT TIMES.

COME, URN'ADO.

YES, MY LORD.

"A BABY WAS COMING. THAT'S WHAT YOUR FATHER TOLD THE KING TWO YEARS AFTER HE MARRIED YOUR MOTHER.

YOU CRY BECAUSE I AM HAVING A BABY?

YOUR CHILD WILL DO MUCH GOOD FOR OUR PEOPLE.

I HAVE BEGUN TO SENSE A CHANGE IN ARDATH, AND IT GRIEVES ME. I WILL TRY TO LEAVE THE KINGDOM TO PALON.

BUT IT IS NOT TO BE SO, FOR ARDATH WILL RULE WHEN I AM GONE.

THAT'S WHAT THE PROPHECY SAID.

I WILL TELL PALON OF THE SECRET ENTRANCE, THE ONE THROUGH WHICH OTAME CAME TO OUR REALM.

THE PROPHECY NEVER SAID WHAT WOULD HAPPEN TO PALON.

FATHER, THERE ARE SECRETS. IF I AM TO BE KING, YOU MUST TELL ME SO I CAN HELP OUR PEOPLE. PLEASE, FATHER.

DO NOT BE AFRAID, MY SON. DEATH SERVES A PURPOSE, AS DOES THE LIFE WE CHOOSE TO LIVE.

FEAR YOUR CREATOR, NOT YOUR CIRCUMSTANCES.

FEAR FOR THOSE THAT DO WRONG, NOT THOSE WHOSE TIME TO PASS FROM THIS WORLD...

...HAS COME.

YOU WILL TELL ME EVERYTHING OUR FATHER HAS TOLD YOU, PALON. EVERYTHING.

FATHER.

"KING VORATHIN DIED THAT DAY."

WITH THE PASSING OF KING VORATHIN, THE FATE OF ARGON FALLS WAS NOW SEALED.

WITH URN'ADO BY HIS SIDE, THE PEOPLE PROCLAIMED ARDATH AS THEIR KING. THEY HAD TURNED AWAY FROM PRINCE PALON.

BUT WHY?

PALON IS THE GOOD BROTHER.

THANK YOU.

SO, WHAT HAPPENED NEXT?

"PALON DID NOT SAY A WORD. HE KNEW THE REST OF THE PROPHECY. HE KNEW WHAT WOULD HAPPEN NEXT.

"STILL, CLAYTON AND OTAME HAD A DECISION TO MAKE. IT WOULD BE ONE OF THE MOST DIFFICULT THEY WOULD EVER MAKE.

"THEY WOULD HAVE TO MAKE IT...

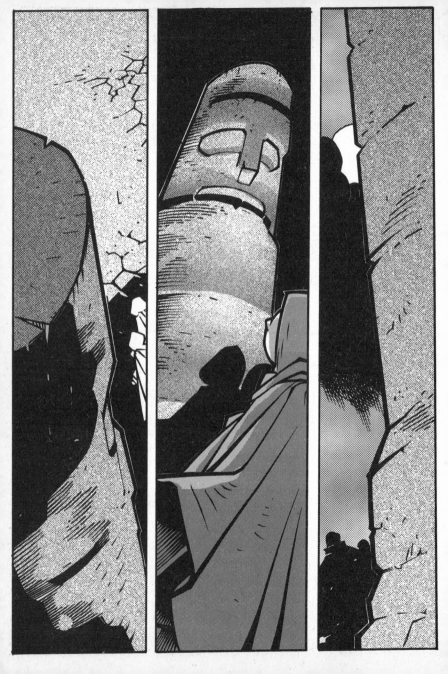

I HAVE A NAME FOR OUR CHILD.

I WOULD LIKE TO CALL HER HANA, AFTER MY MOTHER.

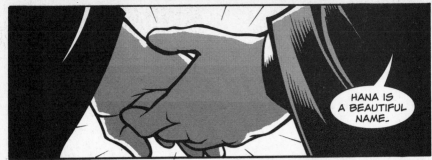

I CAN-NOT GO, OTAME. ARDATH MIGHT FIND YOU IF I DON'T HELP PALON. I PROMISED THE KING THAT I WOULD GET YOU TO SAFETY.

NOOO! IF YOU STAY, YOU'LL DIE. WHAT ABOUT THE PROPHECY?

BUT YOU WILL LIVE, AND SO WILL OUR CHILD.

I LOVE YOU, OTAME.

NO, CLAYTON, NO.

I LOVE YOU SO MUCH.

SO THAT'S HOW I GOT MY DOG.

WHAT HAPPENED TO MY FATHER?

"YOUR FATHER RETURNED TO THE CASTLE.

PALON... PRINCE PALON.

PRINCE PALON?

... WE TRIED TO ESCAPE... BUT THE STONE GUARDIANS...

THEY...

ARDATH?

AND WHAT OF YOUR WIFE AND HEIR?

... THE STONE GUARDIANS THEY... HELP ME!

I'M SORRY FOR YOUR LOSS. BUT A KING CANNOT BE CONCERNED FOR ONE, ONLY FOR THE GOOD OF THE MANY.

"THE CASTLE NURSES TOOK CARE OF YOUR FATHER, WHO HAD ALLOWED HIMSELF TO AWAKEN THE STONE GUARDIANS.

"HE KNEW THAT NO ONE WOULD BELIEVE THAT HE HAD LOST YOUR MOTHER IF HAD NOT BARELY ESCAPED HIMSELF.

"AND SO, BECAUSE OF THE OUTCRIES OF THE PEOPLE WHOSE THOUGHTS WERE TURNED TO POISON BECAUSE OF THEIR NEW-FOUND DISCONTENT, PRINCE ARDATH BECAME KING OF ARGON FALLS.

"IT WAS AROUND THIS TIME THAT YOUR MOTHER GAVE BIRTH TO A LITTLE GIRL.

"HANA.

"STILL, YOUR CHILDHOOD WAS NOT WITHOUT ITS PLEASURE OR FUN."

THERE MUST BE SOMETHING YOU CAN TELL ME ABOUT MY FATHER.

OTHER THAN THAT HE DIED BEFORE I WAS BORN.

WHEN YOU ARE THIRTEEN YEARS OLD, I WILL TELL YOU EVERYTHING, HANA.

BUT THAT'S A WHOLE YEAR AWAY.

"AND, OF COURSE, WITH ME."

WHY DIDN'T MY MOTHER EVER TALK ABOUT YOU, GRAND-FATHER?

I WAS ANGRY WITH YOUR MOTHER. SHE WAS MISSING FOR SOME TIME, AND I FEARED THE WORST. A MONTH HAD PASSED AND THEN ONE DAY SHE RETURNED.

SHE TOLD ME SHE WAS GOING TO HAVE A BABY, AND I WANTED TO KNOW WHO THE FATHER WAS. SHE NEVER TOLD ME.

WE ARGUED. I TOLD HER SHE HAD SHAMED OUR FAMILY, AND THEN SHE LEFT. I DIDN'T FIND OUT UNTIL MUCH LATER THAT BY LEAVING, SHE WAS PROTECTING THE ONES SHE LOVED. I MADE A MISTAKE, AND I KNOW GOD HAS FORGIVEN ME. I AM YOUR GRANDFATHER, AND I WILL DO EVERYTHING I CAN TO PROTECT YOU.

YOU ARE THE PROTECTOR, HANA. IT IS YOU. THIS HAS ALL BEEN BECAUSE YOU WILL BE GREAT. A HERO.

I HOPE SO.

SOMETIMES WE DON'T HAVE ALL THE ANSWERS WE NEED, AND THAT IS WHEN WE LEARN TO TRUST AND TO STEP OUT IN FAITH.

ARE THOSE THE WORDS MY FATHER SAID THAT MY MOTHER WAS NOT READY TO HEAR?

YES, AND YOU ARE NOT READY, EITHER.

I SAID IT BEFORE. I AM FILLED WITH HOPE, BECAUSE DESPITE THE DEATH OF YOUR PARENTS---

---REGARDLESS OF THE LOSS OF YOUR REPUTATION AT SCHOOL---

---EVEN THOUGH YOU HAVE BEEN INNOCENT, YET ACCUSED OF GREAT WRONG---

---YOU CONTINUE TO HOPE.

AND THESE "TESTS" HAVE PROVEN THAT YOU ARE READY FOR ALL THE ADVENTURE TO COME.

WELL, I'M GLAD IT'S NOT FOR NOTHING.

NOT FOR NOTHING? HOW ARE YOU DOING IN YOUR ENGLISH CLASSES, HANA?

WELL, I HAVEN'T BEEN GOING LATELY.

ONE OF THE HIDDEN GRACES OF BEING SUSPENDED.

YEAH, I MEAN WHY CHEAT INSTEAD OF JUST DOING THE WORK AND STUDYING, YOU KNOW?

YEAH, IS GETTING A GOOD GRADE THAT HARD?

BUT THAT'S JUST IT. SHE DIDN'T HAVE TO CHEAT. SHE STUDIED ALL THE TIME.

MY TWO BEST FRIENDS DID IT. I THINK THEY STOLE THE ANSWERS TO THE TEST AND MADE IT LOOK LIKE IT WAS HANA. I DON'T THINK THEY LIKED HOW MUCH TIME I WAS SPENDING WITH HER.

I HAVE TO TELL MY TEACHER WHAT HAPPENED.

IT'S NOT ENOUGH FOR YOU TO CLEAR HANA'S NAME.

YOU HAVE TO BE CONCERNED FOR THE WELL-BEING OF THE OTHER GIRLS AS WELL.

ISN'T THAT WHAT HANA WOULD WANT?

YES.

TORCH IT. BURN IT ALL.

THERE'S MORE TO TELL, HANA, LIKE HOW I BROUGHT THE SWORD HERE FROM ARGON FALLS.

YEAH, ABOUT THAT. IF THOSE CREATURES CAN ATTACK US HERE, THEY MUST HAVE FOUND THE ARCHWAY MY FATHER DIED TO KEEP SECRET.

YES. YOU ARE RIGHT, HANA.

BUT THE TIME HAS NOT YET COME FOR ALL SECRETS TO BE REVEAL...

...ED.

UHN.

WE MUST HELP HER.

NO. SHE IS READY. WATCH.

WOW.

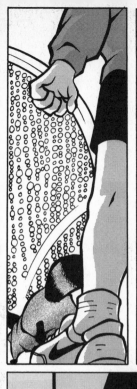

WHERE ARE WE?

THIS IS WHERE WE MAKE OUR PLAN.

PLAN?

PLAN.

TO GO TO ARGON FALLS AND RESCUE MY PEOPLE FROM ARDATH'S REIGN.

THEY ARE YOUR PEOPLE AS WELL, HANA.

TOMO?

YES, HANA?

WHEN WERE YOU GOING TO TELL ME?